THE SECRET CLUB

WRITTEN BY: J P COOK
ILLUSTRATED BY: M P FONSECA

PAGE PUBLISHING, INC.
New York, NY

First originally published by Page Publishing, Inc. 2015

ISBN 978-1-68213-724-6 (hbk)
ISBN 978-1-68213-725-3 (digital)

Printed in the United States of America

This book is dedicated to
my sister Marie. It is with her help
that the fantasy of the
Secret Club was created and
maintained throughout our lives. – JC

Once upon a time, in a faraway place, there lived a little boy and his sister. They were always happy to play games with each other and with their friends too!

They also liked to make up games. Do you like to make up games? I believe that you do too!

One day the brother said to his sister, "Wouldn't it be nice to have a club where only children could be members?"

So the little boy and his sister thought, and they thought and they thought. After thinking for a long time, they came up with an exciting idea.

Their exciting idea was to create a Secret Club. The Secret Club would be special. The Secret Club would have a flag and name badges and would hold meetings.

The brother and sister were so happy and excited talking about the Secret Club that they had trouble sleeping that night.

When morning arrived, the sister and brother woke up and got cleaned up for breakfast and completed their morning chores.

During breakfast they asked their parents if they needed help around the house. Their parents replied, "Thank you for offering to help, but we will be fine today." The children then asked if they could go play.

Their mother answered yes, but before they went outside, they wanted to explain their idea for the Secret Club. Their father said, "What is this Secret Club?" The children began to explain the Secret Club idea.

They said, "The Secret Club is a place for children to gather, and only children can be members." They continued, "But we will need your help and permission first." The little boy and girl then asked, "Please, can we create a Secret Club?" Their mother then said, "The Secret Club sounds interesting. What else will you do in the Secret Club?"

"Well," the children replied, "we take a roll call to record everyone who is at each meeting." The children continued, "We will also promise to follow all of the club rules." Their father laughed and said, "You have rules in your Secret Club too? What are these rules?"

The children remembered all of the rules and repeated them for their parents:

Rule 1: Always tell the truth.

Rule 2: Treat everyone with respect.

Rule 3: Obey your parents.

Rule 4: Always play safe.

The father and mother were pleased to hear the rules for the Secret Club and gave them permission to begin. "Thank you, thank you, thank you," replied the children. "Will you help us get supplies too?" pleaded the children. "Of course," replied the parents. "Just let us know what you need!" The children made a list of supplies for the Secret Club and gave it to their mother.

Next, the brother and sister thought of some ideas for making a meeting place, a flag, and name badges. They soon realized that meetings can be held anywhere. For example, you could hold a meeting in your room.

Your room would then become your clubhouse for the day! You could even hold a meeting between two chairs with a blanket over the top. Now your meeting place is in a blanket tent!

Now that the Secret Club meeting place was ready, the children could now design their flag. First, they practiced on pieces of blank white paper. Then they took a vote for a design that they would use for the flag.

Finally, using their crayons or markers, they drew the special design on a towel that their mother provided. They took their time, because it was their Secret Club flag.

Now, with some help from their parents, the children pressed thumbtacks through the towel into the wooden pole to hold the flag in position.

Finally, they were ready to make their name badges. They printed on a sticker the name of the child who was at their meeting.

When the children finished making name badges, they placed them on their shirts.

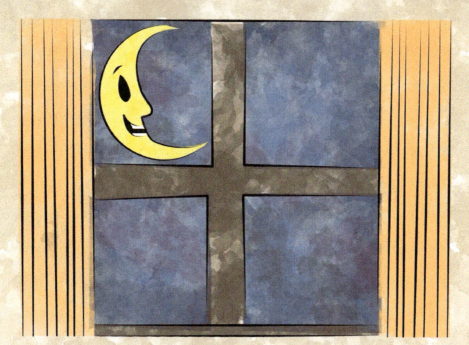

The children then gathered under their blanket tent and held their very first Secret Club meeting. They took roll call and recorded each child's name. They talked and planned and thought about so many things the Secret Club could do, like going on a trip to the zoo for a day. That evening the little boy and girl were so excited about things the Secret Club could do that they could hardly go to sleep.

The children did eventually go to sleep and had the most wonderful dreams!

The end.

CPSIA information can be obtained
at www.ICGtesting.com
Printed in the USA
LVOW05*0006221215
467128LV00020B/89/P